Larry Gets Lost in Seattle

Illustrated by John Skewes
Written by John Skewes and Robert Schwartz

little bigfoot

an imprint of sasquatch books
seattle, wa

J.S.
For Mother and Father

R.S.
For my family, and all our veterans, past and present

A portion of proceeds from this book will be donated to the West Seattle Food Bank.
For more information, please visit www.westseattlefoodbank.org.

www.larrygetslost.com
John Skewes' website: www.retrodyne.net

"Larry Gets Lost in Seattle" and "Larry Gets Lost" ©2007 John Skewes

Manufactured in China in September 2014 by C&C Offset Printing Co. Ltd. Shenzhen, Guangdong Province

Published by Little Bigfoot, an imprint of Sasquatch Books

17 16 15 14   20 19 18 17 16 15 14 13 12

Book design by Bob Suh

Library of Congress Cataloging-in-Publication
Data is available.

ISBN 10: 1-57061-483-0
ISBN 13: 978-1-57061-483-5

Sasquatch Books • 1904 Third Ave, Suite 710 • Seattle, WA 98101
(206) 467-4300 • www.sasquatchbooks.com • custserv@sasquatchbooks.com

**This is Larry. This is Pete.
They ride together in the back seat.**

Because their car wouldn't float,
They drove their car onto a boat.

Washington State Ferries

The ferry boats take thousands of passengers and cars and buses and bikes across the water every day.

Mom and Dad, Pete and Larry,
  Crossed the water on a ferry.
Soon a city was very near;
  The ferry boat docked beside a pier.

Seattle

The Smith Tower used to be the tallest building in Seattle. Look at it now!

Alaskan Way

Smith Tower

Pioneer Square

These are Seattle's oldest buildings, built over 100 years ago.

Pioneer Square was their very first stop,
A real fun place to eat and shop.

Just then, Larry saw a treat!

He quickly bounded  up the street,

But after running several feet...

He realized that he'd lost Pete!

The Underground Tour

You can still see parts of old Seattle underneath Pioneer Square, including the city's oldest toilet!

He searched Seattle's underground,
But the friend he searched for was not around.

Seattle Art Museum

The Hammering Man stands 48 feet tall. He hammers from 7 am to 10 pm every day, except for Labor Day.

He asked a giant if he'd seen Pete that day,
But the giant said nothing. He just hammered away.

He ran past the stadium where football teams meet...

Qwest Field and Safeco Field

**This is where the Seattle Seahawks and the Seattle Mariners play.
On sunny days, the roof of Safeco Field opens up to let the sun shine in.**

To the baseball field right across the street!

He saw some salmon passing by.
Not in the water, but in the sky!

The Space Needle

The restaurant at the top of the Space Needle slowly spins round and round.

**Over his head, a silver train raced,
Toward a saucer that seemed to be from outer space!**

EMP

Here you can learn about music or make your own.

**Even stranger, the bright-colored building next door,
Looked just like a pile of clothes on the floor!**

Not finding his friend was troubling Larry.
In fact, things around him were getting quite scary.

The Fremont Troll

He lives under a real bridge,
and he's holding a real car.

He saw some people
waiting by the street.

But something told him
they couldn't help him find Pete.

Waiting for the Interurban

These statues have been waiting for
the bus since 1979. People like to
dress them up in different clothes.

**Larry then ran through a strange little town,
Built on the water instead of the ground.**

Lake Union Houseboats

Be careful, Larry! That's a sea lion.
They like to visit Lake Washington to
eat the fish.

**Then a big fat creature blocked Larry's way.
Nothing Larry did could make him go away.**

With a running start, Larry leapt...

Landing on a boat where a sea captain slept!

**The captain laughed and picked Larry up.
"Is that your owner, you lost pup?"**

Larry was so excited,
He and Pete were reunited!

The captain called Pete's dad on the phone.
"Don't worry, Larry. You'll soon be home!"

They passed through a gate, and a moment later...

The Ballard Locks

The locks are a big gate that allow boats to go from the lake to the ocean without letting all the water out.

The water dropped like an elevator!

Larry's family was soon within reach.
They agreed to meet at Alki Beach.

Alki Beach

This is Larry's last stop in Seattle, but it's the first place settlers landed and met Chief Seattle, over 150 years ago.

**They fell fast asleep as their car drove away.
It had been quite an unforgettable day.**

Get More Out of This Book

Meet My Town

Because of its rainy climate and unique location on the water, the city of Seattle has a very distinctive "personality." Ask students what sort of personality their town has. How is their town different from Seattle? Does it have beaches, ferry boats, or houseboats? How is it similar to Seattle? Does it have a farmers' market or a baseball field?

One or the Other

Have students write or dictate a short piece comparing the most interesting thing in their town with the most interesting thing in Seattle, based on their reading of the book. Why did they choose the things they did?

Building Blocks

Seattle has some unusual buildings and public structures as portrayed in the book: the Space Needle, the EMP building, the Fremont Troll, the Hammering Man. Ask students to think of any other unusual buildings they've seen or heard about. How would they describe those buildings? Have students design and draw their own "crazy building," show it to the class, and explain how they came up with the idea.

TEACHER'S GUIDE: The above discussion questions and activities are from our teacher's guide, which is aligned to the Common Core State Standards for English Language Arts for Grades K to 1. For the complete guide and a list of the exact standards it aligns with, visit our website: SasquatchBooks.com